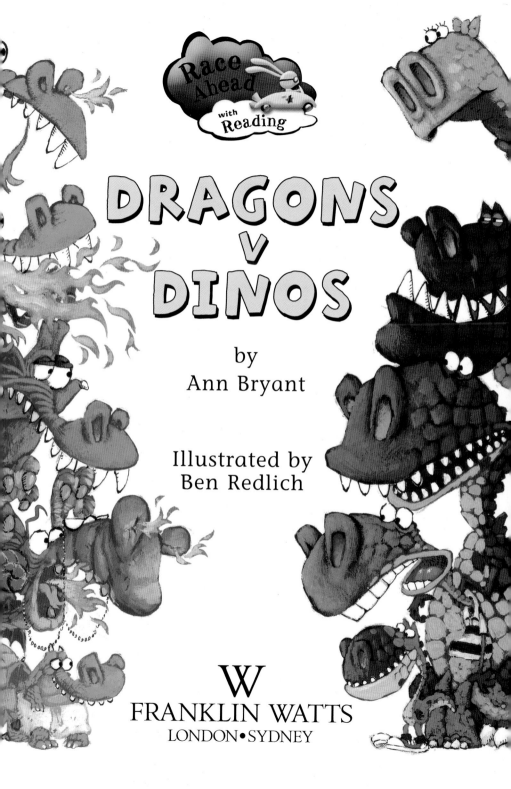

Race Ahead with Reading

DRAGONS V DINOS

by
Ann Bryant

Illustrated by
Ben Redlich

W
FRANKLIN WATTS
LONDON·SYDNEY

Chapter 1

Bobbyraptor had slipped away from the other dinosaurs. He was hiding in the forest high on Scarytops Mountain.

Stamping his feet and thudding his tail, he sent a secret message to his best friend.

He'd hardly finished when he heard

Poppasaurus Rex calling out from below.

"Bobby?

Where are you?

Come on, it's time

for Dragon scaring!"

On the other side of the valley on the Flames-are-Us Volcano, the Dragons were conducting an important meeting. "Your turn to keep watch!" Nanna Dragon informed Dotty Dragon.

"I did it last night," complained Dotty. "Why can't Billyboy do it?"
As she spoke, a lick of fire swished into the cold air, then disappeared in a flash.

"Because he's too young!" snapped Nanna.

"Why do we have to do it at all?"

asked Mumma Dragon, sighing.

Daddio Dragon reared up on his hind legs.

"To warn the others. Then when the Dinos

come we can scare

them silly!"

In the end it was Nanna Dragon who kept

watch. But she soon fell asleep and her loud

snores echoed around the valley.

The Dinos, padding silently down Scarytops Mountain, had to stop themselves from laughing. All except Mummasaurus. "I don't know why we keep doing this," she said, shaking her head. "It's madness!"

"It's fun! We love it!" said Belladocus.

"Dinos at the ready!" Poppasaurus commanded.

"Three, two, one… CHARGE!"

Chapter 2

Instantly, the side of the Dragons'
Flames-are-Us Volcano shook with
the sound of pounding feet as the
Dinosaurs roared up to the top.

"Dino Alert!" screeched Nanna Dragon,
waking with a start. In a flash the Dragons
rose up, flapping their wings and breathing
out bright flames.

"Retreat!" yelled Poppasaurus.

The Dinos thundered back down the

volcano. When they arrived back home,

they sat about sulking.

"That was rubbish!" said Belladocus grumpily.

"Rubbish," the others all agreed.

Bobby waited till no one was watching, then he crept off to the top of the mountain.

On the Flames-are-Us Volcano, Nanna
Dragon was puffing out bright red flames.
"Emergency meeting!" she announced.
"All Dragons to attend. It is time to teach
those Dinos a lesson!"

One by one the Dragons entered the
Great Cave and began to work out
a plan. That night, as soon as it was
completely dark, they silently flew into
the air and swooped off towards Scarytops
Mountain. They giggled to themselves.
The Dinos were in for one
big scare.

13

Chapter 3

The Dragons were hardly over the valley when there came a sharp flash of lightning, followed by a loud clap of thunder.

"Keep going!" ordered Daddio Dragon.

"What's the point?" said Mumma.

"Our fire will be snuffed out when it rains. Let's go home!"

"No, we're almost there!" insisted Daddio.

"Come on everyone!"

But at that very moment the clouds crashed together and lashing needles of rain poured out of the sky. The glowing orange and yellow flames turned instantly to little grey puffs of smoke.

"Ha ha! You've lost your fire!" the Dinos mocked the soggy Dragons above.

"Stupid weather!" the Dragons mumbled under their breath.

Bobbyraptor was high on Scarytops
Mountain, his heart beating excitedly.
"Mummasaurus!" he called.
"Come quickly! I've found something!"

Mummasaurus came to join Bobby in
the woods at the top of the mountain.
"What have you dragged me
up here for?" she asked impatiently.

"Look!" said Bobby, pointing.

Mumma gasped.

"It's a little boy dragon!

Is he all right?

He's very still."

She bent low.

"What's your

name, little one?"

"Titch,"
came the
faint reply.

17

"Well I think you'd better fly back home, Titch," said Mumma. "It's not safe here."

"I can't. I'm too tired," replied the little Dragon in a thin voice.

"Oh dear," said Mumma, looking worried. "What shall we do?"

Chapter 4

On the Flames-are-Us Volcano,
the bright eyes of Mumma Dragon
gleamed in the dark as she flicked
her head this way and that.

"Where's Titch?" she asked the others.

"He'll be around somewhere,"

said Daddio. "Don't worry."

But Mumma Dragon was worried.

Finally, when she'd looked absolutely
everywhere, she slipped away. There was
only one place that Titch could be, and
Mumma was going to save him.

Meanwhile, on Scarytops Mountain,
Mummasaurus had made a decision.
"Come on, Titch," she said. "I'm going
to take you back home."
"I'll come too," said Bobbyraptor.

The little dragon
got up slowly and they all
went down the mountain
into the valley.

Mumma Dragon had a big surprise as she flew over the valley. It looked like three dinosaurs were approaching. One was much larger than the others. And the smallest one seemed to have wings. It was most odd.

"Hey, that's my mumma!" said Titch, looking up. At the top of his voice he called, "Mumma! Mumma!" Then he sunk down to the ground.

Mumma Dragon's eyes flew wide open. "I'm coming, Titch! Don't worry!" she cried. Mumma Dragon flew down and stood face to face with Mummasaurus.

Chapter 5

"Thank you for bringing Titch back safely,"

Mumma Dragon said. "I was so afraid…"

"We'd never hurt a little one," interrupted Mummasaurus. Then she frowned. "To tell the truth, we'd never hurt anyone. Not even a fly. Dinosaurs enjoy roaring and charging about, that's all."

"Same with us," said Mumma Dragon,
her eyes twinkling.
"We like to swoop around
and puff out
fire. It's silly
really."

The two mothers smiled at each other.

Then Mummasaurus began to laugh.

After a moment Mumma Dragon joined in.

They laughed and laughed.

"Are we friends with the Dragons now?" asked Bobbyraptor after a few moments.

"I think we are!" replied Mummasaurus.

"Good!" said Titch Dragon, jumping up and grinning at Bobbyraptor.

"Our plan worked!"

"What?" exclaimed the two mummas.

"We planned the whole thing,"

explained Bobbyraptor.

"We've been friends

for ages!"

"We send each
other secret messages
from our mountain
and volcano!"
added Titch.

"You little monsters!" chuckled Mumma

Dragon. Then she turned to Mummasaurus.

"Why don't you go and get the others.

You're all invited to a party at our place!"

So that was what Mummasaurus did.

And the party was a roaring success!

First published in 2012 by
Franklin Watts
338 Euston Road
London
NW1 3BH

Franklin Watts Australia
Level 17/207 Kent Street
Sydney
NSW 2000

Text © Ann Bryant 2012
Illustration © Ben Redlich 2012

The rights of Ann Bryant to be
identified as the author and Ben Redlich as
the illustrator of this Work have been assert-
ed in accordance with the Copyright,
Designs and Patents Act, 1988.

Series Editor: Melanie Palmer
Series Advisor: Catherine Glavina
Series Designer: Peter Scoulding

A CIP catalogue record for this book is
available from the British Library.

ISBN 978 1 4451 0775 2 (hbk)
ISBN 978 1 4451 0781 3 (pbk)

Series Editor: Melanie Palmer
Series Advisor: Catherine Glavina
Series Designer: Peter Scoulding

Printed in China

Franklin Watts is a division of Hachette
Children's Books, an Hachette UK company
www.hachette.co.uk

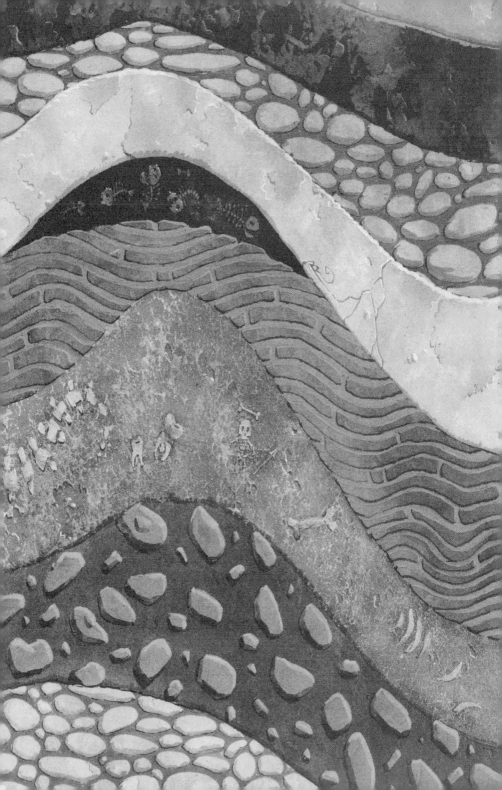